Some hamsters are timid little creatures, frightened of their own shadows, but not Hannibal! When chance throws him headlong into the strange and dangerous world outside his cage, he welcomes the opportunity to explore. The terrifyingly narrow escape from Owl, the friendly advice of Rabbit, the dire warning from Seagull he takes in his stride, learning as he goes along which creatures to trust and which to fear. But at the end of each adventure he is glad when rescue comes and he can return to the comfort and safety of his own home.

Hannibal
on holiday

Story by Raymond Howe
Illustrations by John Berry

Ladybird Books Ltd
Loughborough
1976

HANNIBAL ON HOLIDAY

Hannibal the hamster knew that there was something unusual about the day: both of the children were up before he went to bed.

Being a hamster, Hannibal always slept in the daytime, and woke up at night; but on the first morning of the holiday it was quite impossible for him to settle down. He could almost SMELL the excitement in the air.

"John! Elizabeth! Do get dressed!" said Father. "It will be light in half an hour, and we must make a start as soon as morning comes. We have a long way to travel to the seaside."

Lights were suddenly switched on in every room in the house. Hannibal listened. The family were eating breakfast. There was a clatter of spoons in bowls – and everyone was talking at once.

"We must remember to take Hannibal with us," said Father at last. "He needs a holiday, too."

Hannibal felt his cage being lifted up, and presently it was placed carefully on the back seat of the car. The engine started, and then they were moving away along the road towards the seaside. The holiday had begun!

The car went on – past fields and trees, and green hedgerows; through villages and towns – until finally, they came to the top of a hill, and they saw the sea.

The children lifted Hannibal so that he could see through the car window.

"Look, Hannibal," they said. "Isn't it blue? Isn't it beautiful?"

Hannibal looked. He had never seen so much water. It shone and glittered in the sun, and it stretched away into the far distance, to the place where the sky began.

It happened that the family were staying in a caravan. The caravan stood in a field, and where the field ended there were sand dunes and clumps of tall marram grass. Beyond the sand dunes a long stretch of flat white sand led to the water's edge.

The car was quickly unloaded and all the things taken into the caravan.

"Elizabeth – please bring Hannibal inside," said Mother. "His cage can stand on the floor until we have time to find a proper place for him. But do feed him before you go to the beach."

Elizabeth quickly filled Hannibal's seed tray. But she was in such a hurry to run to the beach, she did not notice as she turned away that the door to the hamster's cage was not quite shut.

In a few minutes the caravan was quiet. Everyone had disappeared. Hannibal was alone.

He stuffed his cheek-pouches full of the grain
that was in his tray. He took several sunflower
seeds – sunflower seeds were his favourite food –
and when he could hold no more, he gave the cage
door a push, and it swung wide open.

Hannibal scrambled out. He ran across the floor
of the caravan, and tumbled outside, falling down
a little step and landing on soft grass.

He picked himself up and blinked several times in the bright sun. Mother and Father were sitting in deck-chairs just outside the caravan door, but they were both asleep.

Hannibal ran towards the nearest clump of marram grass. It offered little shade from the dazzling sun and there was nowhere near at hand that he could hide. He dug himself into the sand and hid his store of food, twitched his whiskers once, and fell asleep.

When Hannibal woke up it was dusk. The tall grass was rustling in the wind. Hannibal pushed his nose out and looked all round. The beach was empty. The sea was far away. He could just hear the swish of the water.

In the middle of the long stretch of sand there was a little wooden hut. Beside the hut many chairs were folded and placed on top of one another. Hannibal decided to move to the hut.

Even if he couldn't get inside, the pile of chairs
would make a good hiding-place. He picked up his
store of food and made his way across the sand.

Presently he arrived in the shadow of the hut.
Moving carefully round the wooden sides, he
discovered a small hole. There was just enough
room for him to squeeze through.
"I wonder who lives here?"
he thought.

Inside the hut it was quiet and dark. Hannibal could see quite well in the dark and he noticed that there were some strange wooden figures sitting on a shelf at the side of the hut. At first Hannibal was frightened. "They look a bit like Elizabeth's dolls," he thought.

They kept very still, and Hannibal soon ceased to be afraid of them.

Suddenly there was a scrambling and pushing
from the hole Hannibal had come through. A small
brown mouse appeared. He was puffing and
panting – far too busy to notice Hannibal. The
mouse was trying to drag a crust of bread through
the hole after him. But the crust was too big.

"Let me help," said Hannibal. "We need to
nibble a bit off this side, I think. Then it will be
small enough to go through."

The mouse let go of the crust. "Goodness! I
didn't know you were here," he said. "Who are
you?"

"I'm Hannibal," said Hannibal. "I'm a hamster.
Who are you?"

"I'm a mouse," said the mouse. "A Punch and
Judy Mouse, to be exact."

They nibbled the crust until it was small enough
to pass through the hole.

"What do you mean, Punch and Judy Mouse?"
asked Hannibal.

"It's quite simple," said the mouse. "This hut
belongs to the Punch and Judy Man. He gives a
show every day."

17

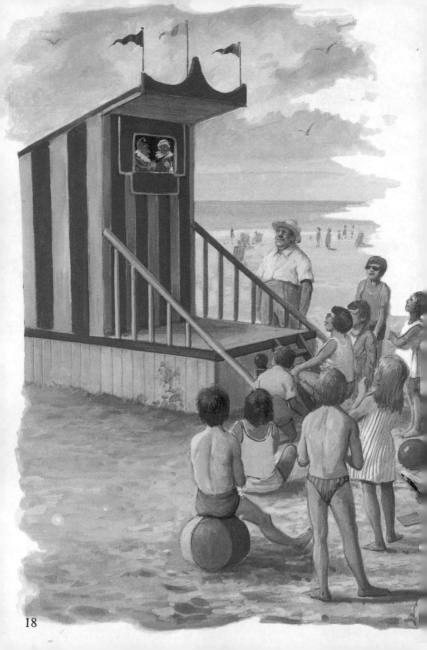

"Show?" asked Hannibal.

"Yes, with the dolls. They are not really dolls, they are puppets, with a space in them for the Punch and Judy Man to put his hand inside and work them. And children come to watch – they often leave sandwiches and sweets on this part of the sand. That's how I get my living."

"I understand now," said Hannibal.

"You will see a show tomorrow, if you stay here," said Punch and Judy Mouse. "Would you like to stay?"

"Yes, please," said Hannibal.

19

Hannibal stayed with Punch and Judy Mouse all that night. The mouse introduced him to the puppets. "That one is Punch," he said. "And that one is Judy. Then there's the Policeman, and the Baby, and the Crocodile. They're all in the show."

In the morning, when the sun was high in the sky, the Punch and Judy Man returned. He set all the chairs up round the front of the hut, and presently children began to come and sit in them.

Hannibal and the mouse hid away.

The show was very noisy. Mr Punch turned out to be quite wicked, and he hit poor Judy several times on the head with his big stick; the Crocodile almost ate the Baby, and the Policeman came along just in time too.

Every time Mr Punch appeared, the children hissed and booed, and when the Policeman came everyone cheered. At last the Crocodile was dead, Mr Punch was dragged off to Jail by the Policeman and the show was over.

"I shall be very busy now," said Punch and Judy Mouse. "There is food to collect when the children have gone. Will you be moving on?"

"Yes," said Hannibal. "I would like to see the great water."

"The great water is very dangerous," said Punch and Judy Mouse. "Strange creatures live there. The water is salt and bad to drink. Watch out for Seagull."

"Who is Seagull?" asked Hannibal.

"Seagull is a huge bird," said Punch and Judy Mouse. "He prefers fish, of course – but I have never trusted him. He would eat a mouse, perhaps . . ."

"I will be careful," said Hannibal.

"If you ever need a friend, remember me," said Punch and Judy Mouse. "Goodbye."

Hannibal started off towards the sea. He scampered along quite happily on the smooth sand. Very soon he came to a place where the sand ended and a patch of shingle began. He was picking his way carefully between the stones, when there was a sudden swish! of wings, and a bird landed on the shingle just in front of him.

Hannibal was startled. He blinked his eyes and twitched his whiskers in alarm.

"Are you Seagull?" he asked.

"No," replied the bird. "I am called Turnstone."

"What an unusual name," said Hannibal. He was very glad that the bird seemed to be friendly.

"Yes," said Turnstone. "I have this name because I earn my food by turning over the stones on the shore. I feed upon Sand Hoppers and other small creatures who hide under the stones."

The bird jabbed down among the pebbles with his strong bill, gave a sudden flick of his head, and turned one of the stones over. Several tiny Sand Hoppers scattered, trying to escape. Turnstone gave a flick! flick! with his bill – too quickly for Hannibal to follow – and the poor creatures were gobbled up in an instant.

"When the water leaves the shore, it is a good time to feed," said Turnstone. "But the sea will come back soon, and you must excuse me now. Goodbye."

Turnstone lifted his wings and flew. Hannibal saw his bright orange legs and his clean white underparts as he went. His wings flashed black and then white as he flew, but when he landed again, further along the shore, he blended so well with the colours of the rocks and sand around him, that Hannibal could no longer see him.

Turnstone had disappeared.

Hannibal moved forward again. He soon came to the end of the beach, where the rock-pools began. The water in the pools was wonderfully clear. Hannibal wandered along a sandy path which led him to several rock-pools. Sea anemones waved their delicate tentacles in the water, and some bright periwinkles were feeding on fronds of seaweed. He caught glimpses of small fish scudding quickly between shells and pebbles which lay on the bottom of the pools. Many of the rocks were covered in green seaweed, and some had limpets clinging to them.

Suddenly Hannibal turned a corner and came face to face with Crab.

Crab was the strangest animal Hannibal had ever met. He had a hard round shell, two huge claws, and legs which carried him along sideways.

Hannibal and Crab stared at one another, standing quite still on a large white rock.

"Stay where you are, Land Animal," said Crab. He clicked his claws together. "Why have you come to the great water?"

Hannibal spoke up bravely. "I came to see the pools," he said. "A friend told me about all the strange creatures who live in them. I mean you no harm."

Crab lowered his claw. "I'm really quite a small crab," he said. "I'm sorry if I frightened you."

"You're a very fine crab," said Hannibal. "What fearsome claws you have!"

"They're only half grown," said Crab. "When many tides have turned, they will be much larger."

"What is a tide?" asked Hannibal.

"Tides make the great water flow," said Crab. "It is a mystery. Even the huge crabs who live in the deep seas cannot explain the tides. Tides moved before there was life in the sea."

He started to move away. "I must go now," he said. "The great water is already returning to the shore."

Crab made a scraping noise on the rock as he walked. "Beware the tide's turning," he said. "When the sea returns, these rocks will be covered. Goodbye."

Whatever did he mean, thought Hannibal, looking round. The edge of the sea seemed to be very far away. He could hardly hear the sound of the waves breaking on the sand. He found a small hollow in the rock. The sun had warmed the stone, and now Hannibal felt lazy. He curled himself inside the hollow, twitched his whiskers once, and fell asleep.

There was a splash! Hannibal woke up suddenly. Great waves were breaking over the rock-pools. The sea had returned.

Hannibal scrambled out of his sleeping-place. The path he had followed from the beach was already under water. He climbed higher up the rock. There was one small stony track which was still dry. Perhaps it would lead him back to the land.

Hannibal ran for his life. He was soon soaked in spray from the breaking waves. As he came to the higher ground, a huge foaming wave almost covered him. He felt the sand give way under his feet and he heard the swish of the water. Then the wave fell backwards, down to the sea. Hannibal was safe.

Just as he was dragging himself further up on
the dry sand, feeling wet and weary and very
frightened, the wide wings of Seagull cast their
shadow over him.

Hannibal stood quite still. He forgot his fear of
the water.

Seagull looked down at the tiny hamster. "I was
flying above the rocks," he said. "I saw that the
tide was coming in. I called, but you were fast
asleep. Are you lost?"

"Yes, I am," said Hannibal meekly.

"Do not be afraid, Land Animal," said Seagull. "I will not harm you. Where have you come from?"

"I came from the Punch and Judy hut," said Hannibal.

"I will guide you back," said Seagull.

He rose on his wide wings. "Follow me," he called. "It is not far."

Hannibal followed. Seagull hovered over the paths between the clumps of marram grass, and soon Hannibal came back safely to the Punch and Judy hut.

"Thank you," said Hannibal, as Seagull soared away.

"It is nothing." The voice of Seagull came drifting back on the wind. "In the winter, when the great storms come, I go to live on the inland fields. Winter is a hard time for all wild things. One day I may need the help of a Land Animal. Goodbye."

Hannibal was glad to see Punch and Judy Mouse again, and to be warm and safe once more.

They had a good meal together, and Hannibal soon felt better. He told Punch and Judy Mouse all that had happened to him. "Now I must ask you to help me," he said at last.

"Of course," said Punch and Judy Mouse. "What can I do for you?"

"I must find my people again," said Hannibal. "They have come to stay for a time in the field where the little houses stand on wheels."

"We will speak to Donkey in the morning," said Punch and Judy Mouse. "He is very wise. He will know what to do."

NEXT SHOW

42

Donkey was huge, but very gentle. In the daytime he carried the children on his back and gave them rides up and down the beach. He had two large ears and he listened carefully to all that Hannibal said to him.

Then Donkey gave his advice. "You must go to the shopkeeper," he said. "The shopkeeper has a special window in his shop. Messages are written there for people to read. If *your* people are still living in one of the little houses on wheels, they will read the message and come and collect you."

Donkey flicked his ears. "You must go alone," he said. "If the shopkeeper finds a mouse in his shop, he may trap him and kill him."

"Thank you for your advice," said Hannibal. "Goodbye."

That night, Punch and Judy Mouse set off with
Hannibal towards the shop. "I will show you the
way," he said. They left the shadow of the hut, and
the stack of chairs. A bright moon was shining
over the beach, and the light made a silvery path
across the sea. When they reached the grassy field,
Hannibal turned and looked back. "The sea is very
wonderful," he said. "I shall remember it always."

They moved together through the lines of
caravans. There were a great many caravans in the
field, and they all looked exactly the same to
Hannibal. It was quite impossible to say where his
own family were living. Perhaps they had gone
home already!

The shop stood in the middle of the field. It was

a big wooden building, much larger than the Punch and Judy hut, and there was a light shining from one of the windows.

"I can go no further," said Punch and Judy Mouse. "I do hope you find your family."

"Thank you," said Hannibal. "Goodbye."

Hannibal found a split in the wood below where the light was shining, and he squeezed himself through.

Inside the shop, the shopkeeper was setting out his shelves. He was a little man, with a kind face. He wore spectacles, and his head was bald and shiny.

Hannibal ran quickly across the floor of the shop, where the light was brightest.

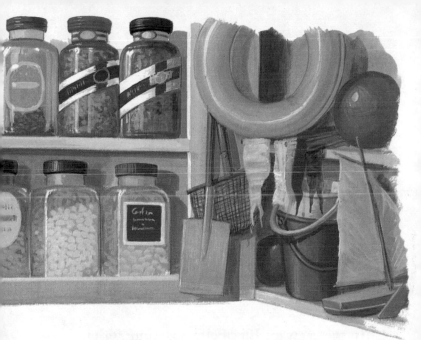

"Well, well," said the shopkeeper, as he picked Hannibal up. "I wonder where you have come from? There's sand in your coat, and salt, too." He peered at Hannibal over his spectacles. "Perhaps I'd better find a box to put you in for tonight," he said. "Tomorrow I will put a notice in my window."

In the morning, the shopkeeper wrote out a clear notice on a piece of white card, and placed it in the shop window.

FOUND – ONE HAMSTER
OWNER PLEASE APPLY WITHIN.

In the caravan, Elizabeth was quite forlorn. "Hannibal has been lost for two days and we'll never find him now," she wailed. "He's probably drowned."

At that moment her brother John came back from the camp shop. "Do cheer up, Elizabeth," he said. "Come along with me. I've something to show you."

The children went back to the shop. Elizabeth read the notice again and again. She could hardly believe it. "I wonder if it really is Hannibal?" she said.

"We'll soon see about that," said John.

49

"Hannibal! It *is* you!" cried Elizabeth. "I'm so glad we've found you again."

They thanked the shopkeeper for his kindness, and then they carried Hannibal carefully back to the caravan and put him into his cage. For the rest of the holiday he stayed in a sunny window, sleeping in the daytime and waking up at night. Sometimes, on quiet nights, he could hear the sound of the sea.

He thought of his friend Punch and Judy Mouse. He thought of Turnstone and Crab and Seagull and Donkey, and all the wonderful things he had seen among the rock-pools.

There came a day when the holiday was over. The car was packed and the family were ready to leave the seaside.

Father lifted Hannibal's cage. He gave the hamster a hard look, then he winked.

"My word," he said. "What adventures you must have had."

"It's a pity he can't talk," said Mother. "If he could speak to us, he would tell us all about it."

But Hannibal felt quite sleepy. He was suddenly very glad to be going home.

He yawned, twitched his whiskers once, and fell fast asleep.